E TORRES
Torres, Leyla, author.
Lost kitten

D0125239

To my cousin, Margarita, for her love and dedication to rescuing lost kittens. –LT

To my husband, Oriol and my little daughter Maria, who wants a kitten now. –ÁR

Reycraft Books
55 Fifth Avenue
New York, NY 10003
Reycraftbooks.com

Reycraft Books is a trade imprint and trademark of Newmark Learning, LLC.

Copyright © 2019 by Reycraft Books, an imprint of Newmark Learning, LLC

All rights reserved. No portion of this book may be reproduced, stored in a retrieval system, or transmitted in any form or by any means, electronic, mechanical, photocopying, recording, or otherwise, without written permission from the publisher. For information regarding permission, please contact info@reycraftbooks.com.

Educators and Librarians: Our books may be purchased in bulk for promotional, educational, or business use. Please contact sales@reycraftbooks.com.

This is a work of fiction. Names, characters, places, dialogue, and incidents described either are the product of the author's imagination or are used fictitiously. Any resemblance to actual persons, living or dead, is entirely coincidental.

Sale of this book without a front cover or jacket may be unauthorized. If this book is coverless, it may have been reported to the publisher as "unsold or destroyed" and may have deprived the author and publisher of payment.

Library of Congress Cataloging-in-Publication Data is available.

ISBN: 978-1-4788-6867-5

Illustration credit: Ángeles Ruiz

Author photo courtesy of Leyla Torres
Illustrator photo courtesy of Ángeles Ruiz

Printed in Guangzhou, China
4401/0919/CA21901484
10 9 8 7 6 5 4 3 2 1

First Edition Hardcover published by Reycraft Books

Reycraft Books and Newmark Learning, LLC. support diversity and the First Amendment, and celebrate the right to read.

THE lost Kitten

Dad plopped the grocery bag on the kitchen table.

Over it fell and everything came

tumbling

out...

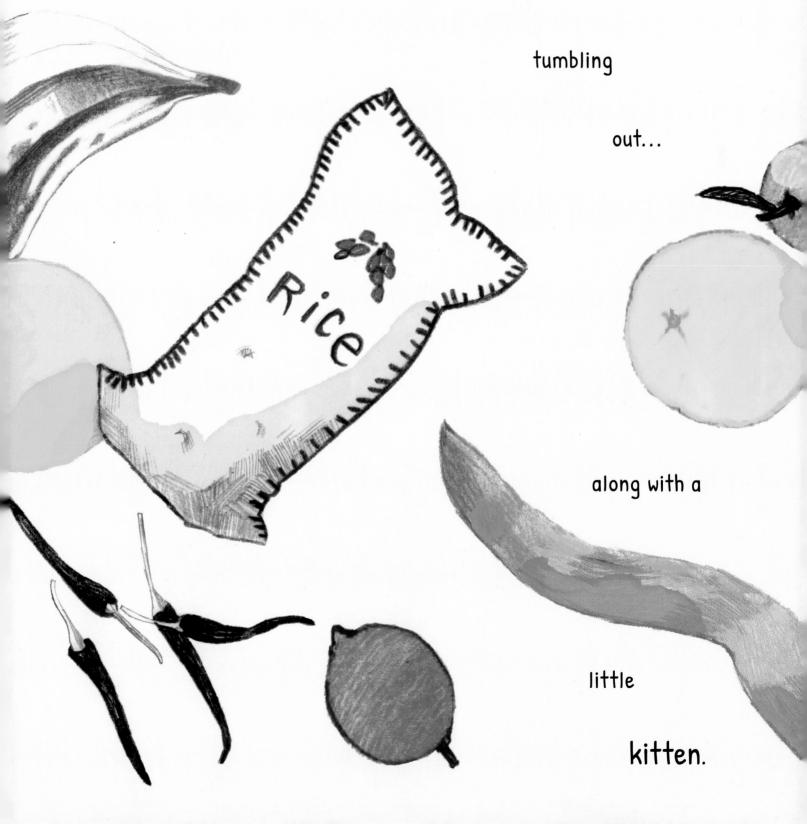

Rice

along with a

little

kitten.

"Papa, I didn't know they sold orange kittens at the grocery store!" I said.

The kitten's fur was softer than cotton and its tail stuck up straighter than a flagpole.

"He was outside our door," said Papa. "He's clean and looks well-fed. He must belong to one of the neighbors."

"Purrrrr, purrrrr"

The kitten made a noise!

"That means he likes you," said Papa.

"I think it means he's hungry," I said.

"I have the perfect thing," Papa said. "How about a plate of chicken and rice with saffron? Our leftovers from dinner."

As I watched the kitten eat, I thought about all the things we could do together.

"CAN WE KEEP HIM?" I ASKED.

Papa's left eyebrow went up, like it always does when he's thinking too much.

"Sweetie, the kitty must have an owner," said Papa.

"Okay Papa. But if he doesn't have an owner,
CAN WE KEEP HIM?"

"We will see what Mama says," said Papa.

So we put the kitten in a cardboard box
and went to knock on doors.

First, we rang the bell at Mrs. Azucena's house.

"Does this kitten belong to you?" I asked.

"No, Emilia," she answered. "This kitty isn't mine.
But let me give you a blanket to keep him warm."

I put the blanket over the kitty.

"Papa, do you think we

CAN KEEP HIM?" I ASKED.

"No, sweetie," said Papa. "We need
to keep looking for his owner."

Next, we knocked on Mr. Evan's door.

"Does this kitten belong to you?" I asked.

"No, Emilia, this little fur ball isn't mine," said Mr. Evan. "But how about a stuffed mouse for him to play with?"

The kitten batted the toy mouse around the box.

"Papa, do you think the kitten

CAN STAY WITH US NOW?" I ASKED.

"No, whoever lost him might be looking

for him right now," answered Papa.

Ding, Dong!

The bell rang through the next house.

"Does this kitten belong to you?" I asked.

"No, Emilia," Mrs. Romano said. "Our kitten is black and white. But take this can of tuna for him."

I added the can to the box.

"Papa, this has to mean something. Now we have
a blanket, food, and a toy for him!"

"CAN HE LIVE WItH US, PLEASE?" I BEGGED.

Papa's left eyebrow went up. He was thinking again.
So we walked to the next house.

We lightly rapped on Mrs. Manuela's window.
"Mrs. Manuela, did you lose this kitten?" I asked.

Tap, tap, tap!

Next, Papa walked to the Cruzes' house. I hoped no one would open the door. Then my friend Nathan hopped out onto the steps.

"I like dogs," he said. "But take this." He threw a ball of yarn into the box.

Our box was getting so full, the kitten could barely fit.

"CAN WE tAKE HIM HOME NOW?"

Mama was waiting at the door when we got home.

"Look, Mama, we found a lost kitty!"

"CAN WE KEEP HIM?"

That's when I saw a small boy
and a lady just behind Mama.

"This is Luis. He has lost his kitten," said Mama.

I looked at the boy. The boy looked at me. I closed my eyes tight and stretched out my arms.

Luis looked into the box and frowned.

"THAt's NOt MY LOst KIttEN!" HE SAID.

Suddenly, the kitten purred. "That means
he likes you," Luis said.

"That means he's hungry," I said, laughing.

I ran into the kitchen and got the rest
of the chicken and rice with saffron.

"What's his name?" Luis asked.

"He doesn't have one yet?" I said. We watched the kitten gobbling up the chicken and rice with saffron.

"Purrrrr,"
purrrrr"

"SAFFRON!"

We both shouted. Saffron seemed to agree.

Then he stretched out and took a nap.